GW01090489

What Colour Is Love?

JOAN WALSH ANGLUND

What

Colour

Is

Love?

COLLINS ST JAMES'S PLACE LONDON

ISBN *0 00 193380 9*

Copyright © 1966 by Joan Walsh Anglund

First published in Great Britain 1967

Fourth Impression 1973

Fifth Impression 1974

Printed in Great Britain

Collins Clear-Type Press: London and Glasgow

for adele and sydney
with gratitude and love......

An apple is red.

The sun is yellow.

The sky is blue.

A leaf is green.

A cloud is white . . .

and a stone is brown.

The world has many things . . .
the world has many people . . .
the world has many colours . . .
and each of them is different.

In a garden
all the flowers are different colours,
but they live happily together . . .
side by side.

In a forest
    all the birds are different colours,
    but they live happily together . . .
    side by side.

In a meadow
    all the animals are different colours,
    but they live happily together . . .
    side by side.

In our world
   all the people are different colours,
   and, sometimes, they live happily together . . .
   side by side.

Colours are important
    because they make our world beautiful,
    but they are not as important
        as how we feel . . .
            or what we think . . .
            or what we do.

Colours are "outside" things
and feelings are "inside" things.

Colour is something we see with our eyes,
but love is something we see with our heart.

An apple is red,
the sun is yellow,
the sky is blue,
a leaf is green,
a cloud is white . . .
and the earth is brown.

And, if I asked you,
could you tell me . . .

what colour is love?